It's Mine!

Tracey Corderoy   Caroline Pedler

Good Books

Intercourse, PA 17534, 800/762-7171, www.GoodBooks.com

Lulu had come to play
with Baby Bear.

"I'm playing tigers with Rory," said Baby Bear.

"I *love* tigers!" cried Lulu. "Can I play?"

"Oooh, yes!" Baby Bear smiled.

"Look, I've made a den!"

"I can roar louder than you!" giggled Lulu.
"Raaghh!"
"Raaghh!" roared Baby Bear. And they roared and roared and *roared*.

Suddenly Baby Bear's tummy rumbled. "We need tiger-snacks!" he said. So he hurried off to find some.

But when he came back...

…Lulu was playing with Rory!

"Wheeee!" giggled Lulu, with a big tiger grin.

"Lulu! Stop!" cried Baby Bear. "Rory doesn't *like* swinging!"

Baby Bear grabbed
Rory's leg. Lulu held
on tight.

   "But…Rory's…*mine!*"
puffed Baby Bear.

Baby Bear tugged.
Lulu tugged back *until…*

CRASH!

Then Lulu
started to cry.

"Baby Bear!" said Mommy, hurrying in.
"You need to *share* your toys."

Slowly, Baby Bear held out another toy for Lulu.

"But I don't want *him*," Lulu frowned. "I want *Rory*."

"Why don't we go to the park?" smiled Mommy. "I'll bring Rory along with *me*."

"Okay," mumbled Baby Bear and Lulu.

At the park, Lulu stomped to the seesaw
and Baby Bear plodded to the swings.

But Lulu's seesaw wasn't
much fun. It wouldn't go up and down.
   Baby Bear's swing wasn't much fun either.
It wouldn't go forward and backward!
   After a while, Lulu wandered over
to Baby Bear…

"I can push you if you like," she said.
"Yes, please!" smiled Baby Bear.
Lulu pushed the swing, a little
at first. Then higher and higher
and higher!

"*Wheeee!*"
chuckled Baby Bear.
And *then* he had an idea.

Baby Bear scrambled off
the swing and dashed
across to Mommy.

"Lulu! Lulu!" he cried,
racing back…

"*You* hold Rory," said Baby Bear. "He says
he *loves* swinging now!"

"Let's push him together!" Lulu smiled.

"Or I could push all *three* of you," said Mommy,
"so you can *share* the swing."

"Higher! Higher!"
they giggled.

"Time to go!" said Mommy at last. "I've got
a treat for you at home..."

"*Ice cream!*" cheered
Baby Bear and Lulu. Then they
both sang…

"Friends together—one, two, three…
Sharing ice cream, you and me!
Drippy, soft, and yummy, too,
Some for me and some for you!"

For my lovely niece, Jemima ~ T. C.

For twins, Hallie and Dylan, and a lifetime of sharing ~ C. P.

Copyright © 2012 by Good Books, Intercourse, PA 17534
International Standard Book Number: 978-1-56148-766-0
Library of Congress Catalog Card Number: 2012000184

Text copyright © Tracey Corderoy 2012
Illustrations copyright © Caroline Pedler 2012
Original edition published in English by Little Tiger Press,
London, England, 2012
LTP/1800/0383/0312 • Printed in China

Library of Congress Cataloging-in-Publication Data
Corderoy, Tracey.
It's mine! / Tracey Corderoy ; Caroline Pedler.
p. cm.
Summary: Baby Bear loves to play with his friend Lulu, but gets upset
when he sees her being rough with his favorite toy, Rory.
ISBN 978-1-56148-766-0 (hardcover : alk. paper) [1. Sharing--Fiction.
2. Bears--Fiction. 3. Toys--Fiction.] I. Pedler, Caroline, ill. II. Title. III. Title: It is mine!
PZ7.B7649Ism 2012
[E]--dc23
2012000184